Snort!
OINK
CLACK!
OW!
WAH
OUCH!
TAP!
BAA!
M
Splash!
THUD!
scratch!
ack!
BOP!
ZAP!

Who's That Banging on the Ceiling?

Colin McNaughton

TWA
BLEE
WHAC
Huff!
ont!
Slurp!

WALKER BOOKS
AND SUBSIDIARIES
LONDON · BOSTON · SYDNEY · AUCKLAND

SLAM!
DOP!
YOW!
Miaow
Zap!
Screech!
CLATTER!
Crunch!
Bon
BANG!
Arrghh!
Clang!
PAR

STIRLING LIBRARIES
3804803 0289255
D0335493

For Françoise, Ben and Tim

First published 1992 by Walker Books Ltd
87 Vauxhall Walk, London SE11 5HJ

This edition published 2013

2 4 6 8 10 9 7 5 3 1

© 1992 Colin McNaughton

The right of Colin McNaughton to be identified
as author/illustrator of this work has been asserted by him
in accordance with the Copyright, Designs and Patents Act 1988

Printed in China

All rights reserved. No part of this book may be reproduced,
transmitted or stored in an information retrieval system in any form or
by any means, graphic, electronic or mechanical, including photocopying,
taping and recording, without prior written permission from the publisher.

British Library Cataloguing in Publication Data:
a catalogue for this book is available from the British Library

ISBN 978-1-4063-4736-4

www.walker.co.uk

Home Sweet Home!

"What's that clack, clack, clacking
on the ceiling?" says Mrs Manky
on the ground floor...

"It sounds like a dinosaur dancing the fandango!"

But that would be silly!
"What's that boing, boing, boinging?"
says Mrs Fettle on the first floor...

"It sounds like elephants on pogo sticks!"

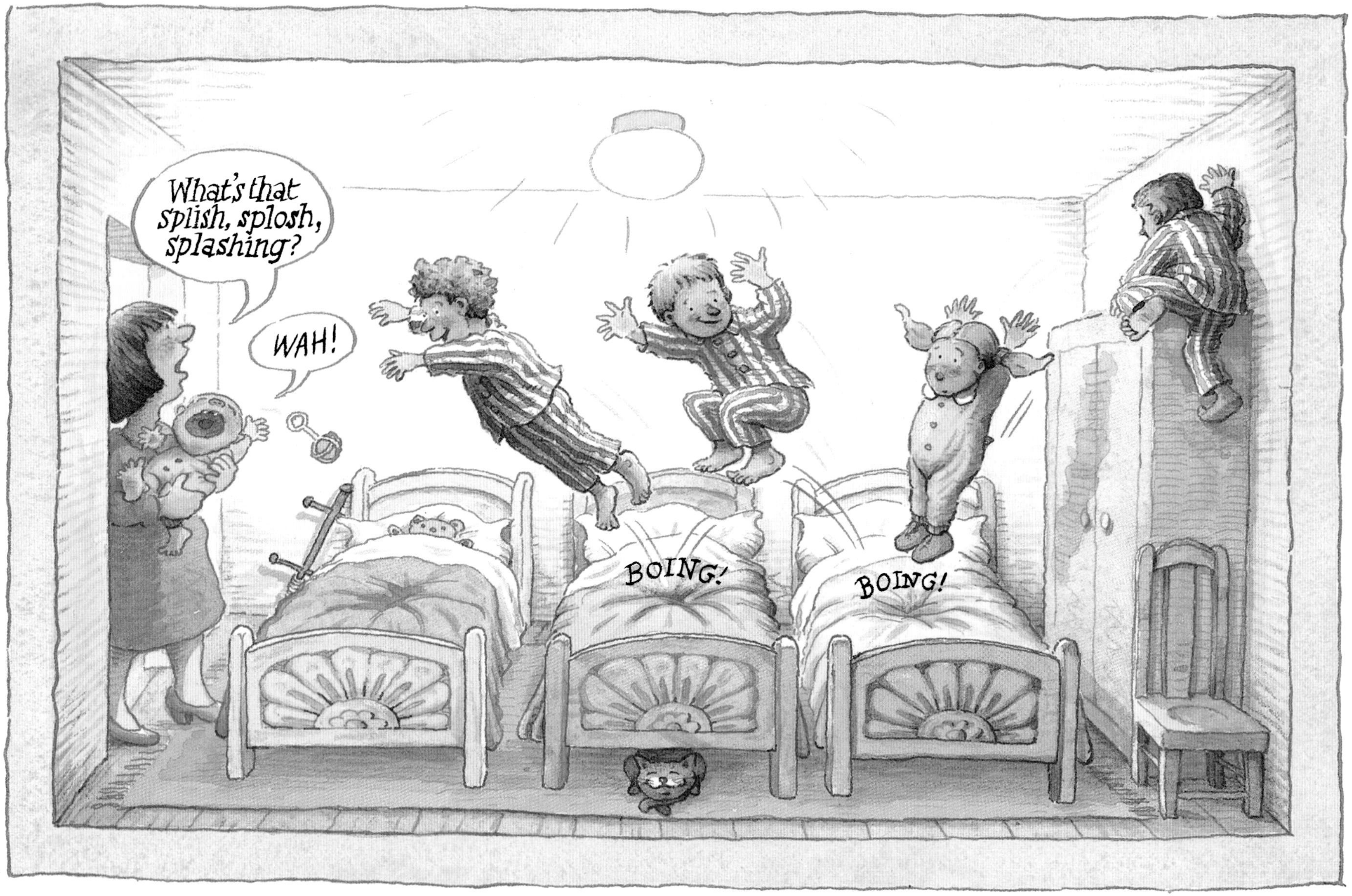

But that would be silly!
"What's that splish, splosh, splashing?"
says Mrs Dutz on the second floor...

"It sounds like a sea battle!"

But that would be silly!
"What's that grunt, snort, slobbering?"
says Mrs Gowk on the third floor...

"It sounds like a pigsty!"

But that would be silly!
"What's that squeak, squeak, squeaking?"
says Mr Clarts on the fourth floor...

"It sounds like giant mice!"

But that would be silly!
"What's that crash, boom, twanging?"
says Mrs Tarly-Toot on the fifth floor...

"It sounds like a rock and roll show!"

But that would be silly!
"What's that moo, cluck, quacking?"
says Mr Plodge on the sixth floor...

"It sounds like a farmyard!"

But that would be silly!
"What's that ow, ouch, yowing?"
says Mrs Haddaway on the seventh floor...

"It sounds like a fight!"

But that would be silly!
"What's that argh-ee-argh-ee-arghing?"
says Mr Chebble on the eighth floor...

"It sounds like Tarzan of the Apes!"

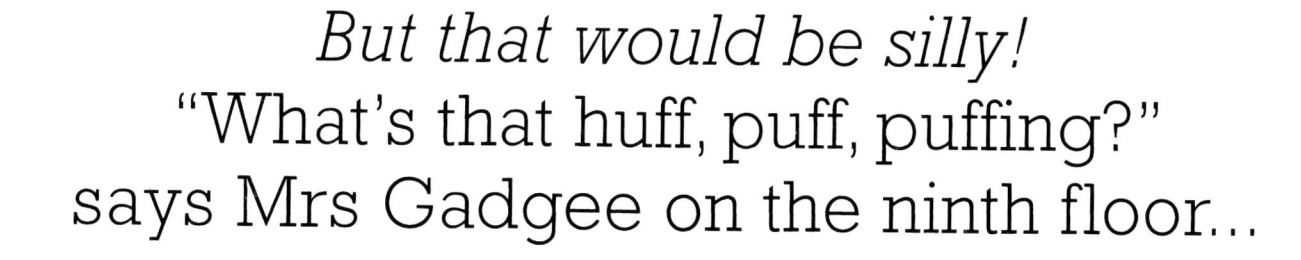

But that would be silly!
"What's that huff, puff, puffing?"
says Mrs Gadgee on the ninth floor...

"It sounds like the big bad wolf!"

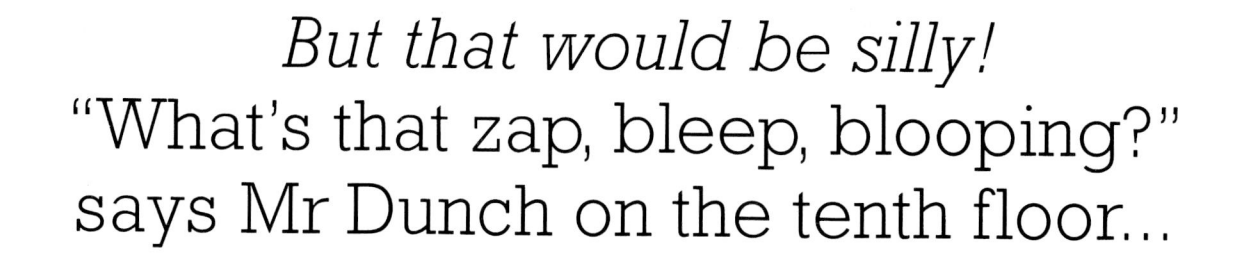

But that would be silly!
"What's that zap, bleep, blooping?"
says Mr Dunch on the tenth floor...

"It sounds like an alien invasion!"

But that would be silly!
"Who's that banging on the ceiling?"
says Mrs Hacky-Mucky on the top floor...

"It sounds
like King Kong
tap-dancing!"

The End!